Cat Tales

The Cat with Two Names

Cat Tales

The Cat with Two Names

LINDA NEWBERY

Illustrated by Stephen Lambert

For Matthew and James Goddard

This edition first published in the UK in 2008 by Usborne Publishing Ltd.,
Usborne House, 83-85 Saffron Hill, London EC1N 8RT, England.
www.usborne.com

A CIP catalogue record for this book is available from the British Library.

FMAMJJASOND/09 87704 ISBN 9780746096147 Printed in Great Britain.

Chapter One

Once, Cat had a name, but after a few weeks as a stray he forgot what it was.

He'd had a home once, and a cat-flap, and a basket to sleep in. Not any more. One day his owners packed up and left. Without Cat. They didn't want him.

New people moved into the house,

blocked up the cat-flap and shooed Cat away. They didn't want him either.

What would he do? It was winter, and the nights were long and cold. There was no warm kitchen to sleep in, no bowl of food put down for him.

He'd have to learn to survive.

Cat became very good at hiding. He found a place underneath bushes for sleeping when it was wet, and a shed roof for sprawling on sunny days. He had places for walking and places for stalking; he knew places where no one could find him.

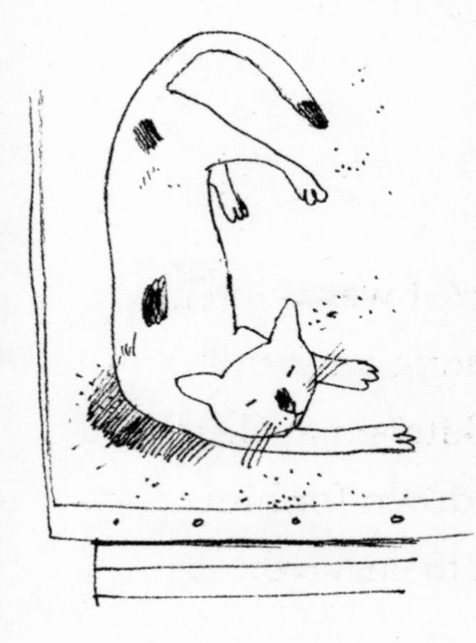

At night, he prowled around the dustbins looking for food. He lurked around the gardens, searching for scraps in compost heaps, hoping for bits of bread that had fallen off bird-tables.

Sometimes, when he was very brave or very hungry, he went through some other cat's cat-flap and took food from a kitchen.

Once he got into a fight with Ginger Flash, who lived in the house on the corner and didn't want anyone else in his territory. Ginger Flash, a tough fighter, tore Cat's ear and made it bleed. Cat felt very sore and bruised after that fight, and didn't even feel like looking for food.

What really made Cat's fur bristle and his claws tighten was the way Ginger Flash changed into a sweet, purring pussy-cat the instant his owner came to the door to call him inside. Ginger Flash's owner didn't call him Ginger Flash. She called him Fluffball.

"Here, Fluffball! Dinner's ready!" she would call from the back door.

At once, Ginger Flash stopped hissing and growling, and looked as sweet as a kitten. His back arched, ready to be stroked. He trotted to the back door and rubbed himself against his owner's legs. Then he went inside and stuffed himself with food, all the delicious flavours that Cat could remember - cod and salmon, special meaty chunks with gravy, pilchard-flavoured biscuits.

Cat had peeped in once, and seen Ginger Flash's luxury dining area.

Ginger Flash had his own mat, labelled PUSS. He had two food bowls of his own – one for meat, one for biscuits – a saucer of water and a saucer of milk. Cat's mouth watered, just thinking about it. He remembered having his own food bowl, and being called indoors at meal-times.

Not any more.

Cat especially hated Ginger Flash's smug way of coming outside to wash his paws and whiskers when he'd finished eating. But at least Cat was safe at those times. Ginger Flash was so full of meat and biscuits and milk that he'd waddle off for a good sleep on a car bonnet before he thought about fighting again.

Then, one day, in the darkest, coldest time of winter, Cat found Rose.

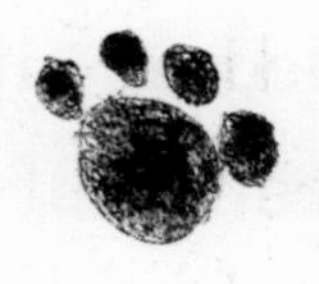

Chapter Two

Cat had been dreaming about warm radiators and airing cupboards. When he woke up, under his bush, he was so cold that he curled up and tried to get back into his dream. But it was no good. Hunger growled in his stomach and drove him out to find food.

It was a frozen morning, so frosty that

the grass crunched under his paws. Today the dustbins were emptied, and there was always the chance that someone might have left a lid open or dropped something on their way out to the pavement.

Then:

"Wwrrrwwrrraaa - owwWWWW!"

It was Ginger Flash, yowling from under a parked car. Cat saw slitty green eyes, flashing with spite.

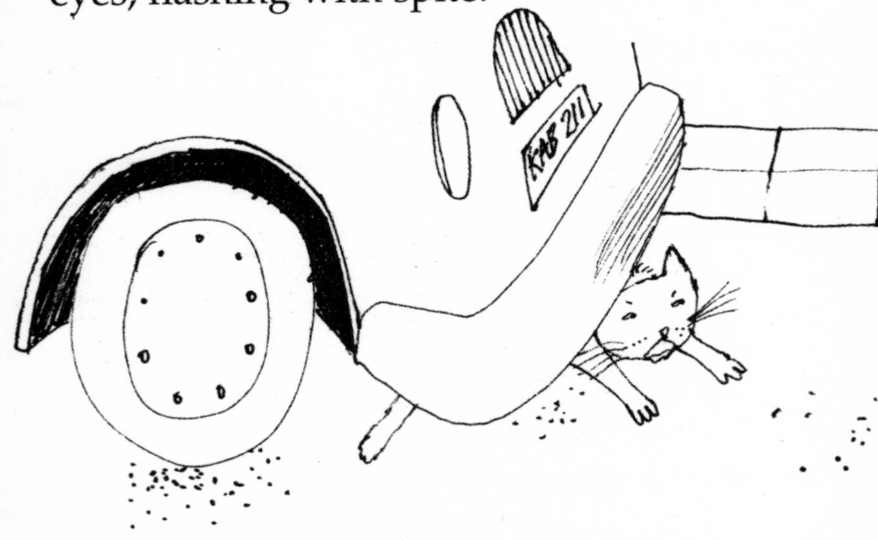

Cat stretched himself on to his paw-tips to make himself tall. His fur bristled all the way along his spine, and he felt his tail bush out like a toilet-brush. He didn't wait for the ginger flash, for the needle-sharp claws and teeth – his ear was still sore from last time.

He gave one small, frightened yowl, and then he ran.

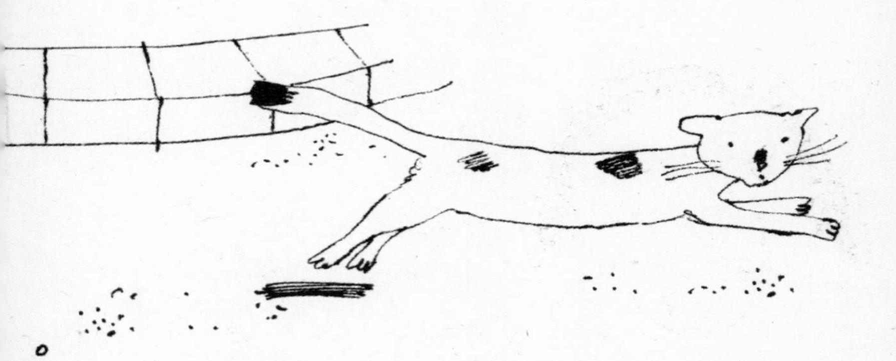

He skittered.

He hurtled.

Along the pavement, through garden hedges, round the back of a garage, up a fence, down again to the dark space behind a shed. He crouched there panting, with his ears sharply pricked for any sound of Ginger Flash.

He heard nothing but birds cheeping. He was safe here. Now that he was out of Ginger Flash's territory, Ginger Flash

would leave him alone and go back to his under-car sitting.

Cat crept out. He'd run so far that he wasn't sure he'd ever been in this garden before. There was a frozen fishpond, crisp frosted grass, a bird table. And a delicious smell.

Cat's whiskers twitched.

Bacon rind.

Cooked.

The warm, salty smell of it was so wonderful that he started to drool. He crouched beside the shed and watched the birds squabbling. Starlings and sparrows flapped their wings and argued, balancing on the table as they tried to snatch the best bits of bacon and fried bread.

Cat waited for what he hoped would happen, and soon it did – two starlings, having a tug-of-war over a strip of bacon, both let go at once in a flurry of wing-beats and squawking. The bacon strip whirled into the air and flumped down on the grass.

Cat slunk out before any of the birds dared to fly down for it. They shrieked their alarm calls and rose from the table in a panicking blur of wings. Delicately, he picked up the bacon rind in his teeth. He'd carry it back behind the shed and eat it where no one could see him.

If he were really lucky, the birds would drop another piece.

Then, from the open back door, he heard:

"Here, puss-puss! Come here, kitty-cat!"

Cat ran as fast as he could without dropping the rind. Behind the shed, he bolted down the bacon so fast that he hardly tasted it.

The voice was still calling:

"Come back, puss-puss! I won't hurt you!"

It was a woman, round-faced and

red-haired, well-wrapped up in a coat and scarf. Her voice was kind. Cat ventured nearer. She was crouching, holding out a hand to stroke him.

It was a long time since he'd been stroked. He couldn't resist. He crept closer.

"Oh, you poor thing! You look half-starved! Let's get you some food and a saucer of milk, Smudge-Face."

And that was how he met Rose, and got one of his names. Smudge-Face, Smudge for short.

Chapter Three

Rose and Smudge got on very well together. Smudge had two meals a day, and milk and biscuits, and everything a cat could want. He even had his own chair to sleep in.

The only problem was that there wasn't much *time* for sleeping, in Rose's house. Although Rose lived by herself,

she had a sister who came to visit, bringing her two children.

Often, Darren and Daisy would come by themselves, while Rose's sister was at work. All of them – Rose, Rose's sister, and the children – were full of energy and ideas.

They all loved cats. Especially, they loved energetic cats. They liked the sort of cats who were always chasing round after ping-pong balls, and

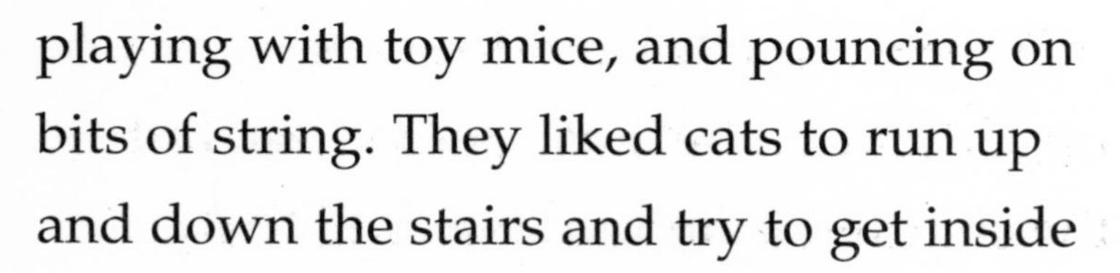

playing with toy mice, and pouncing on bits of string. They liked cats to run up and down the stairs and try to get inside the duvet covers. They liked cats who scaled the apple trees and tight-rope-walked the branches.

Smudge batted and swiped, pounced and sprang, rolled and cuffed and clambered till he was worn out, but the children always wanted to play more games.

"Where's the ping-pong ball?" Darren would ask.

"No, let's get him to play with this squeaker!" Daisy would answer.

Smudge didn't want to seem ungrateful, so he'd always join in. But the children didn't understand that sometimes a cat just needs to sleep.

One day he was so tired that he gave up trying to sleep in the house. Trying very hard not to be seen, and enticed into some lively new game, he crept to the very back of Rose's garden, looking for a quiet place to curl up.

Darren and Daisy, thinking he was playing hide-and-seek, joined in.

"Smudge! Smudgy-Face! We're coming to find you!" they yelled.

Smudge decided that he wasn't going to be found until tea-time. He crawled under the quince bush and suddenly there it was – a hole in the fence. It wasn't a very big hole. It was just big enough for Smudge to fit through.

Keeping a wary ear and eye out for Ginger Flash, he slunk under another lot of bushes and came out on a lawn, in another garden. At the far end of the lawn was another house.

Smudge could hear a man humming to himself, round by the dustbin. The back door stood open. Smudge crept closer and looked inside. He could see that no cat lived here, because there was no mat, no food bowl, no saucer of milk. There was, however, a rather nice chair. A chair with a very tempting, squashy, cushiony seat.

Smudge tiptoed into the kitchen and jumped up on the chair. He curled himself up and crossed his paws over his face, shutting his eyes tightly.

He was so tired that he didn't even run away when the man came back into the kitchen and shut the door.

And that's how he met Wilfred, and became the Cat with Two Names.

Chapter Four

Life became very busy, now that Smudge had two homes, and two people to attend to.

When he was feeling energetic, he went to Rose's. When he was feeling sleepy, he went to Wilfred's.

Wilfred, who was usually working in his study, left a window open so that

Smudge could get in. Wilfred didn't call him Smudge, of course. He called him Fungus.

"Ah, Fungus!" he would say, when Fungus appeared at the window. "I was wondering where you were! How are you today?"

You might be thinking that Fungus is a strange name to choose for a cat, but

Wilfred loved fungus of all sorts, shapes and sizes. He was in the middle of writing a book about mushrooms and toadstools. He spent a lot of time wandering round fields and woods looking for specimens, a lot of time staring at them through a microscope and a lot more time typing at his computer.

Wilfred had lived alone since his wife died, and was very pleased to have Fungus for company. He wasn't at all bothered that Fungus didn't want to run around or play games.

Fungus settled in very happily. There was a comfortable rocking-chair in Wilfred's study, where he could sleep for hours while Wilfred worked.

Now he had a routine worked out.

- *Breakfast number one at Rose's*
- *Breakfast number two at Wilfred's*

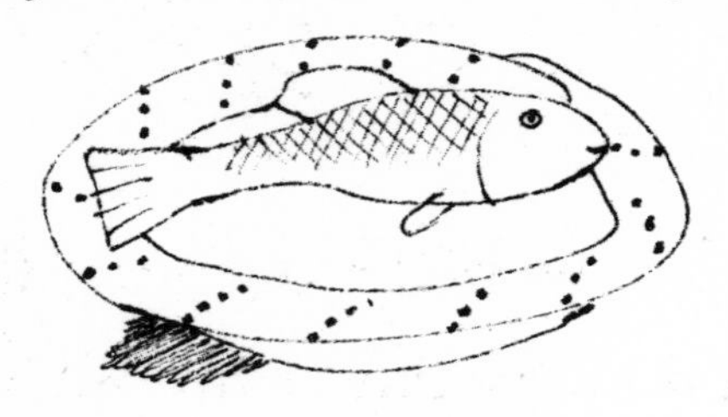

- *Sleep in Wilfred's rocking chair*
- *Elevenses at Rose's*
- *Twelvses at Wilfred's*
- *Milk and a snack at Rose's*
- *Games with Daisy and Darren*
- *Milk and lunch*
- *Rest at Wilfred's*

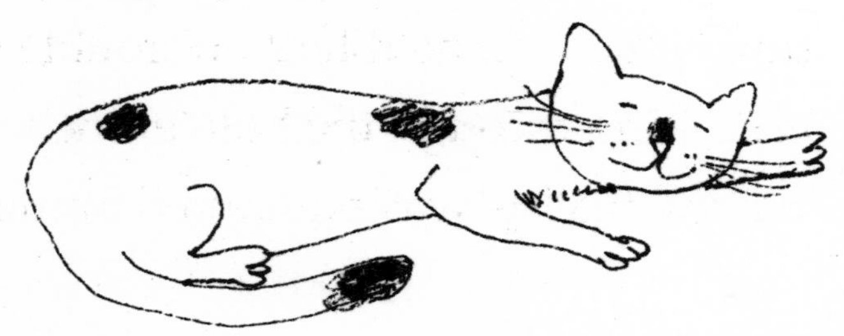

- *Supper number one with Rose*
- *Supper number two with Wilfred*
- *Rest*

At Rose's, he had a different flavour of cat food every day, with pilchards on Saturdays. At Wilfred's, he ate tinned food during the week and flaked cod on Sundays. When Wilfred was getting on particularly well with his book, they had cream.

Fungus began to get rather plump.

When he'd been skinny unloved unwanted Cat, he'd had no trouble at all getting through the hole in the fence.

Now that he was pampered Smudge

and well-fed Fungus, it was more difficult. To squeeze through, he had to breathe in very deeply and concentrate very hard.

And he had to remember to change his name, too, each time he came through the fence.

Then one day, Smudge-Fungus got himself into very serious trouble. Very serious trouble indeed.

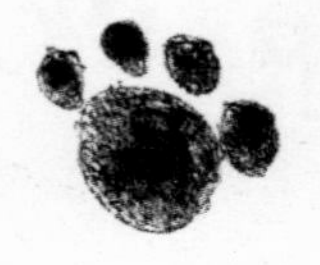

Chapter Five

Smudge-Fungus could never resist an open door.

It was nearly summer, and the people who lived two doors along from Rose were bringing their garden chairs out from the garage.

Smudge-Fungus went along to investigate.

He'd never seen so much clutter in a garage. There certainly wasn't room for a car. There were pots of paint, and rolls of wallpaper, and garden chairs, and boxes of old books. There were Christmas decorations, and curtains, and a barbecue, and carrier bags stuffed full of other carrier bags. There were things stacked in corners and piled on top of each other and

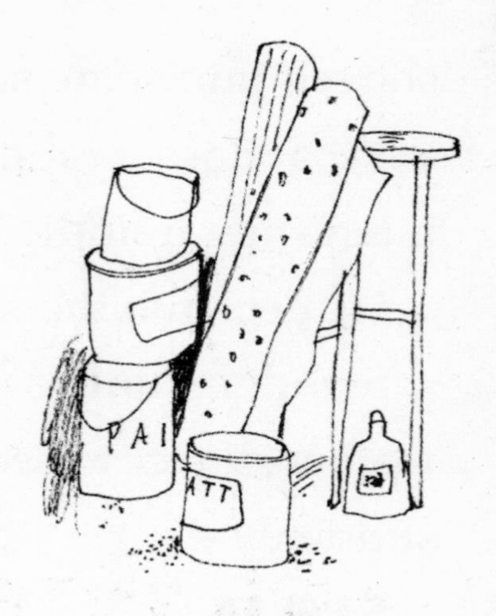

shoved into spare spaces.

What does a cat do when he sees an interesting muddle?

He gets into the middle of it.

Smudge-Fungus was pawing at an old feather-duster to see if it could fly when suddenly –

SLAM.

The garage doors were slammed shut.

And locked.

Smudge-Fungus blinked.

It was dark in the garage, and the only light came through a crack between the doors.

He tried scrabbling at the door with his paws. Nothing happened.

He tried miaowing. Nothing happened.

FRAG
TEA

He tried yowling.

Then he heard a car engine start up, and the car moved away.

He was trapped.

Chapter Six

"But where's Smudge?" Darren said, outside Rose's house. We haven't even seen him today!"

"We can't go home without saying goodbye to Smudge," Daisy said.

"He's most probably prowling about in the garden, or up the apple tree," Rose said. "Don't you worry about Smudge."

But when her sister's car had pulled away and she'd waved to the children and gone back indoors, Rose began to think hard.

She hadn't seen Smudge since breakfast time. He'd eaten his breakfast, washed himself, gone outside, and she hadn't seen him again since. Rose got Smudge's tea ready for him and then stood at the back door, tapping a fork against the edge of his dish. Smudge never missed a meal.

"Here, Smudgy-Face! It's tea-time! Sardine flavour, your favourite! Here, Smudgy-Face!" she called.

Nothing. Not a miaow, not a scrape of claws on the garden fence.

This was most odd. Rose started to feel worried. She called and called, but there was no Smudge.

Wilfred had had a good day's work. Someone had brought him a marvellous specimen of *boletus luridus*, and he'd typed up several pages of his book.

"Right then, Fungus, old chap," he said, not turning round from his desk. "I think we deserve a special treat, don't you? What would you say to a glass of whisky for me, and a saucer of milk for you? Fungus? Wake up!"

He turned round in his seat.

No Fungus.

Wilfred got up and felt the cushion. Not even warm.

He stood there, rubbing his chin, thinking hard.

He'd seen Fungus this morning, first thing; Fungus had guzzled a whole saucer of milk. He thought Fungus had settled down to sleep in the rocking-chair, but he couldn't be sure now.

"I know what I'll do," he said to himself, going through to the kitchen. "Meaty chunks with gravy. That'll fetch him."

Fungus never missed a meal.

“Fungus! Fungus!” Wilfred called from the back door. “Dinner is served! Let me recommend the chef’s succulent meaty chunks, served with savoury gravy, specially seasoned for the discerning cat’s palate!”

Nothing.

“Fungus! Fungus!” Wilfred shouted.

Nothing.

This was really worrying. After he’d checked the garden twice, Wilfred found his front door key and went out to search…

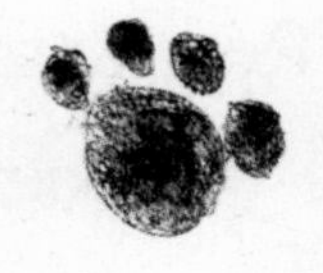

Chapter Seven

…and met…

Rose, coming the other way. She'd looked in every front garden, up every tree, down every alleyway.

"Excuse me," Rose said. "I'm looking for my cat. Have you seen him? White with black patches and a smudgy nose."

"What a very strange coincidence!"

Wilfred said. "Because I'm looking for *my* cat. His name's Fungus and he's white with black patches too."

"Mine's called Smudge," Rose said. "You don't think they could have run off together, do you?"

"Hmm. I don't think so. Fungus is such a quiet, home-loving cat," Wilfred said.

"Then let's search together," Rose said.

They walked the length of the road and round two corners into Rose's street, all the while shouting, "Smudge! Fungus! Fungus! Smudge!"

"There's a cat!" shouted Rose, but it was only Ginger Flash, looking very superior as he surveyed them from a wall.

Then Rose had a rather worrying idea. She stopped walking.

"You don't suppose," she said to Wilfred, "that your cat Fungus could have frightened my Smudge and chased him away?"

Wilfred looked most offended.

"I can assure you, madam," he said, "that my Fungus is a kind cat, a perfectly-mannered cat, a gentlemanly cat. He would never dream of doing anything of the sort. Maybe your cat Smudge has lured my Fungus away?"

Rose drew herself up to her full height and looked Wilfred straight in the eye.

"I cannot stand here and listen to accusations against my cat," she said sternly. "My Smudge is the nicest cat you could hope to meet. A playful cat, a mischievous cat, a lively cat. But not a cat to *lure*, as you put it, to *lure* other cats away from their homes."

"Then how is it," Wilfred asked, "that both cats have gone missing?"

They stood glaring at each other.

Then, from a nearby garage, they heard a mournful sound.

"Waowaow – OOWWWWWWW!"

"That's Fungus!" cried Wilfred.

"That's Smudge!" cried Rose.

She marched up to the house door and banged the knocker.

Wilfred went to the garage door and pressed his ear to the crack.

"Don't worry, Fungus!" he called. "We'll soon have you out of there!"

"Wait there, Smudge!" Rose called. "We're coming to let you out!"

Chapter Eight

Smudge-Fungus had got hungry and thirsty, then hungrier and thirstier. When lunchtime came, he thought of the saucer of milk he'd normally have at Rose's. When mid-afternoon came, he thought of the biscuits he'd usually eat at Wilfred's. And when evening came, he thought of the two dinners he'd usually have. Thinking about all this food made his stomach feel emptier and emptier.

He was frightened, too. He'd heard the car drive away. Perhaps those people had gone away for the whole day, or perhaps even for a holiday! Then no one would ever find him.

He did the only sensible thing to be done. He found a pile of old curtains, kneaded them with his paws, turned round in a circle three times and went to sleep.

Then – a while later – he woke up in a strange, dim place, and couldn't remember where he was.

It was dark. It was musty. It was dusty. And he couldn't see how to get out.

His mouth opened, and out came a loud, mournful wail.

"Waowaow - OOWWWWWWW!"

It echoed round the garage like a cat chorus.

The next thing he heard was voices arguing outside. Wilfred and Rose's voices. Then the sound of a car pulling up with a squeak of brakes.

"My cat's locked in your garage!" he heard Rose telling someone.

"No, *my* cat's locked in your garage!" he heard Wilfred objecting.

Then a third voice, sounding puzzled. "How many cats are in there?"

"Just one. Mine," Rose said.

"No, just one. Mine," corrected Wilfred.

"Well, we'll see," said the voice. Smudge-Fungus heard a key turning in the lock, and the doors were thrown open. There, standing in front of the parked car, were Rose and Wilfred, one each side of a strange man.

"That's my cat!" Rose and Wilfred shouted, both together.

Smudge-Fungus hesitated. Who should he go to?

The man solved his problem by picking him up and holding him tightly. "Is this your cat?" he asked Rose.

"Yes. That's Smudge!" Rose said firmly.

The man turned to Wilfred. "Is this *your* cat?"

"Yes. That's Fungus!" Wilfred said firmly.

"I can prove he's my cat," Rose said. "If you look under his chin, you'll see a tiny black spot."

The man looked. There was the spot.

"But I can prove he's *my* cat," Wilfred said. "If you look at his right ear, you'll find there's a scar."

The man checked. There was the scar. He looked from Rose to Wilfred and back again, baffled.

Rose reached out and stroked Smudge's head. He purred.

Wilfred reached out and tickled Fungus under the chin. He purred.

Rose was the first to realize.

"Your garden's the one behind mine, isn't it?" she asked Wilfred. "Have you noticed how fat your cat's getting?"

"Yes, I have," said Wilfred. "But that's because he does nothing but sleep all day. He's the laziest cat I know."

"Oh no, he isn't," Rose said. "He chases ping-pong balls and climbs trees and gallops up and down stairs. If you ask me, he's fat because he gets two breakfasts and two dinners every day, not to mention two lots of elevenses and probably two lots of afternoon tea."

"You mean this is—"

"Yes," said Rose. "This is Smudge AND Fungus."

The garage man still seemed rather confused.

"So whose cat *is* he, then?" he asked.

Chapter Nine

This is what happened.

After all their arguing, Rose and Wilfred went home for a cup of tea at Rose's house. While Smudge-Fungus devoured his late sardine tea, they talked and talked, and discovered that they quite liked each other. Rose had always been very fond of those red toadstools with white spots on them, and Wilfred copied down the recipe for Rose's lemon-and-ginger cake.

Next weekend, Rose went for lunch at Wilfred's house, and they talked and talked some more.

Nowadays, they see each other nearly every day. Walking from Rose's house to Wilfred's, or from Wilfred's house to Rose's, used to take quite a few minutes when they went all the way round by the road, so they decided to enlarge the hole in the fence to make a short cut.

A people-flap, as Smudge-Fungus calls it.

He still lives in both houses, but he doesn't get quite so many dinners, or quite so much cream, and is getting slimmer.

And he only has one name now.

Fudge.

About the author

Linda Newbery loves to write. She also loves her four cats: Holly, Hazel, Finn and Fleur, who keep her busy and who have inspired Cat Tales. Linda had her first novel published in 1988 and she's the author of many books for young readers. She has won the Silver Medal Nestlé Children's Book Prize and the Costa Children's Book Award.

Linda writes in a hut in her garden, usually with a cat or two for company.

Cat Tales

Curl up with Cat Tales from award-winning and enchanting storyteller, Linda Newbery.

The Cat with Two Names

Two of everything sounds perfect, but it soon leads to double the troube for Cat...

ISBN 9780746096147

Rain Cat

Nobody believes that the mysterious cat can control the weather...until it starts to rain!

ISBN 9780746097281

Smoke Cat

Where do the shadowy cats in next door's garden come from and why won't one particular cat join them?

ISBN 9780746097298

Shop Cat

Strange things have started happening in the toy shop since Twister came to stay...

ISBN 9780746097304

And coming soon...

The Cat who Wasn't There

Vincent is so lonely without his cat, Snow... until a slim white cat appears in his garden.

ISBN 9780746097328

Ice Cat

Tom's cat is made of snow and ice, so of course it can't come alive...or can it?

ISBN 9780746097311

For more fun and furry animal stories, log on to www.fiction.usborne.com